AUNT
SEVERE
and the
DRAGONS

AUNT
SEVERE
and the
DRAGONS

by Nick Garlick
Illustrations by Nick Maland

Andersen Press
London

This edition first published in Great Britain in 2010
by ANDERSEN PRESS LIMITED
20 Vauxhall Bridge Road
London SW1V 2SA
www.andersenpress.co.uk
Reprinted 2011

British Library Cataloguing in Publication Data available.

ISBN 978 1 84939 055 2

Printed and bound in Great Britain by CPI Bookmarque, Croydon CR0 4TD

For
Fieke den Hollander
Oodlevrouw Supreme

1
A New Home

When Daniel was eight years old, his parents bought an aeroplane and set off to explore the world. They telephoned every evening to let him know exactly where they were.

But on the ninth evening, the telephone didn't ring. Nor did it ring on the tenth or the eleventh evenings. So on the twelfth day a search party of famous explorers set off at once to find them. The explorers tramped through forests, climbed down into ravines, paddled up rivers and dived to the bottom of the deepest lakes. But they didn't find so much as a scrap of clothing or the tiniest part of an aeroplane.

Daniel's parents had vanished.

And Daniel, who had nowhere else to go, left the house he had grown up in and travelled all the way across the country to live with his Aunt Severe.

2
Aunt Severe

Aunt Severe wasn't her real name, of course. It was actually Great-Aunt Emily – Emily Florence Biddle-Smith. She was his mum's aunt. But Aunt Severe was the name that popped into his head the moment he stepped down off the train and laid eyes on her at the station.

Daniel had only ever met his great-aunt when he was a tiny little baby, so he didn't remember her at all. All he had ever seen were photographs of her at home. In the photos, she was a smiling woman standing in a beautiful garden packed with masses of brightly coloured flowers. Nothing like the gloomy, grim-faced figure who stood there waiting for him with a sign in her hand with his name written on it.

She looked as if she'd never smiled in her life and didn't like any colour except grey. It was the colour of the overcoat that covered her from her chin to her ankles and the colour of the floppy hat that stopped just above her eyes. It was even the colour of the knobbly walking stick she used to jab Daniel's suitcase.

'What's in there?' she demanded.

'My clothes. And some books and toys.'

'Stuff and nonsense!' she harrumphed. 'There won't be any time for stuff and nonsense in my house!'

Without another word, she led him across town to a street lined with tall trees and beautiful big houses. All except for one. Its walls were crumbling. Its windows were cracked. Tiles were missing from the roof and the front garden was full of weeds. This was Aunt Severe's home and it was just as glum and gloomy inside as it was on the outside. Once the door slammed shut, she told him to empty his suitcase, then took all his books and toys and locked them away in a room at the top of the house.

'*If* you're very good,' she said, 'I *might* let you have one book at weekends.'

'But I always read at night!' Daniel protested.

'Nonsense!' said Aunt Severe. 'Night-time's for sleeping.'

She took him to the kitchen and handed him a cold spinach sandwich and a glass of water.

'I don't really like spinach,' he said.

'It's good for you and it's all you're getting!' she replied.

When he was finished, Aunt Severe showed him to his bedroom.

'I get up very early!' she announced as he climbed into bed. 'Very, *very* early!'

The door banged shut. The room was plunged into darkness. Feeling very sad and very, very lonely, Daniel drifted slowly off to sleep.

3
Off To Work

Aunt Severe was as good as her word. She woke him up the next morning at four-thirty, gave him a cold spinach sandwich for breakfast, led him outside and pointed at a rusty wheelbarrow.

'Bring that and follow me,' she commanded.

Off they trudged through the dark, silent streets with Aunt Severe peering intently into the gutter. After three minutes, she stopped dead and with one quick flick of her walking stick sent a filthy old rag covered in mud flying into the bottom of the wheelbarrow. Then, before Daniel could ask what she wanted them for, she had flicked two old paper cups and a plastic bottle on top of the rag, and set off down the street.

On they went through the quiet, sleeping town, with Aunt Severe pausing only to send bottles and cups, rags, scraps of newspaper, empty cans and even an old sock and a shoe with a hole in the toe, flying into the wheelbarrow. By seven o' clock it was full of rubbish and they set off for home.

'Aunt?' said Daniel. 'When we get back, may I play in the garden?'

Aunt Severe was thunderstruck. '*Play?*' she cried. 'When there's work to be done?'

'I thought we'd finished working.'

'Finished? We've only just *begun*. When we get back to the house you're going to wash everything in that wheelbarrow.'

'But it's the school holidays,' Daniel said.

'Excellent,' said Aunt Severe. 'Then you'll have even more time to work for me and earn your keep!'

In her kitchen, Aunt Severe had a huge porcelain sink as big as a bath. She emptied the contents of the wheelbarrow into it. Then Daniel washed and soaped and scrubbed and rinsed, and then washed and soaped and scrubbed and rinsed all over again until Aunt Severe was completely satisfied. She took everything away to a room at the back of the house. When she came back she gave him a cold spinach sandwich for supper, sent him to bed and woke him up at four-thirty the next morning to do exactly the same thing all over again. And the day after that. And all the days of the week until Saturday.

On Saturday, he found out what she *did* with all that rubbish.

4
Rubbish For Sale

The wheelbarrow stood outside the front door. In it were all the cans, cups, bottles and rags they'd collected and washed during the week. But now all the rags had been sewn into six big blankets, the tin cans had been glued together to make trays and the old plastic bottles had been filled with flowers made from all the old newspapers. She'd even glued the handle of a brush to the old shoe with a hole in the toe and called it a watering can.

'What are you going to do with them, Aunt?' asked Daniel.

'Sell them, of course,' she replied, as if it were the most natural thing in the world.

Daniel didn't think anybody would be mad enough to buy such rubbish. And he was right. All the owners of all the houses in all the streets they visited took one look at the junk in the wheelbarrow and went straight back inside their homes without a word.

By the time they returned to Aunt Severe's street, the wheelbarrow was just as full as when they'd started.

Then something odd happened.

The front door of the house right next to Aunt Severe's home burst open and the owner dashed down the path. He wore a green suit, a bright yellow waistcoat and blue bow tie. His moustache curled up at both ends in little circles and a monocle gleamed in his right eye.

'Good afternoon! Good afternoon!' he cried. When he spoke, the ends of his moustache bounced up and down. 'What do we have here?'

'Blankets,' said Aunt Severe. 'And trays and pretty vases. Would you like to buy one?'

'Just one?' said the man, pulling out his wallet. 'Why, I'd like to buy the lot!'

And that was when Daniel saw something that really took his breath away.

5
The Colonel

Standing on the man's front lawn was a statue of a dragon. It was twice as big as Daniel and coloured bright green from tip to tail. It had outspread wings, pointed teeth, gleaming talons and a tail that curled around into a deadly point.

'Wouldn't want to meet one of them when you were all by yourself, would you?' asked the owner. 'What's your name, young fella?'

'Daniel,' said Daniel.

'I'm the Colonel.'

'Are you *just* called Colonel?'

'Yes, indeed.'

'Don't you have a proper name?'

'I used to,' said the Colonel, 'but button my waistcoat, I'm dashed if I can remember it.'

'Not at all?'

'Not for years and years,' he replied. 'I say, would you like to come in for a cup of tea?'

Before Daniel could say, 'Yes', Aunt Severe took his hand and led him away.

'But he bought everything you made,' said Daniel.

'Oh,' said Aunt Severe, 'he always does that. And he always asks me in for tea.'

Daniel was puzzled. 'Don't you ever go?'

Aunt Severe was astounded. 'CERTAINLY NOT!' she boomed. 'I've got far more important things to do than sit around all day drinking tea.'

Daniel was puzzled. 'Aunt, if the Colonel always buys everything you make, why don't you sell it to him first thing in the morning? Then you wouldn't have to spend all day walking round the town.'

'If I did *that*,' replied Aunt Severe, 'then nobody else would have a chance to buy anything, would they?'

'But nobody did buy anything.'

'Don't be irritating,' said Aunt Severe.

She handed him a stick and sent him out into the garden to cut down stinging nettles.

But Daniel didn't want to cut down nettles.

He wanted to play with his toys and read a book. He got so angry that he whacked the oak tree in the middle of the garden and hurled the stick up into the branches.

'Ooowwww!' yelled a voice. 'Watch where you're throwing things!'

Sitting on a branch directly above him were four creatures with scaly wings, long pointed tails and wide yellow eyes that stared into his.

'You're . . . dragons!' Daniel gasped.

'What did you think we were?' snapped one of them. '*Acorns?*'

6
Teachers

Daniel was convinced he was going to be burned to a crisp and eaten, but all the dragons did was look at him. So he looked back. They weren't quite what he had expected dragons to be like.

For a start, they weren't really much bigger than him. He'd always thought dragons were huge creatures, but these looked like he could almost pick them up and carry them. They had two small arms high up on their chests, two big legs under their tails, and wings tucked up neatly on their backs. They were covered from nose to tail in bright red scales and had big dark blue claws.

One of them wore a baseball cap on its right

ear. Another clutched a ragged umbrella, while the third wore a scarf round its neck. The fourth dragon didn't have anything except a bandage wrapped round the tip of its tail and plasters on all its claws. It kept its head down and gazed at the ground with a sad expression.

'Are you going to eat me?' Daniel asked.

'No,' said the dragon with the umbrella, 'we're not going to eat you.'

'Are you going to burn me up?'

'Of course not! Dragons stopped burning people up *hundreds* of years ago.'

'More's the pity,' grumbled the dragon with the baseball cap.

'Oh, don't pay any attention to him,' said the dragon with the umbrella. 'He's always in a bad mood. Now, my name is Gilbert. I'm the leader of the group.' The other dragons snorted at that but Gilbert ignored them. 'The dragon with the scarf is Filbert. She's the clever one. She knows how to read. The dragon with the baseball cap is Zilbert. He looks after us. And last—'

'I'm always last,' muttered the fourth dragon.

'—is Dud,' continued Gilbert. 'Actually, his real name's Dudley.'

'But we call him Dud,' Zilbert said, 'because that's what he is. A dud.'

Dud's eyes drooped. His shoulders slumped. He let out a long, sad sigh.

'My name's Daniel,' said Daniel. 'Where did

you get those things you're wearing?'

'Oh,' said Gilbert, 'we found them at the back of your house when we arrived.'

'I thought so,' said Daniel, who recognized them as part of the rubbish he'd wheeled home yesterday. 'You'd better not let Aunt Severe see them.'

'Who's Aunt Severe?'

'My great-aunt. She's very strict. If she knows you took those things from her wheelbarrow, she'll be furious.'

The dragons exchanged glances.

'Sounds just like our teachers,' Filbert said.

'Teachers?' said Daniel. 'Do dragons have *teachers*?'

'Of course we have teachers,' Zilbert snapped. 'That's one of the reasons we ran away from school in the first place.'

7

Lessons, Lessons, Lessons

Daniel couldn't believe his ears. 'Dragons have to go to school?'

'Of course dragons have to go to school,' said Zilbert. 'Don't *you* have to go to school?'

'Yes,' said Daniel. 'But I'm only eight.'

'Well, we're only thirty,' said Filbert.

'But that's old!'

'Not for a dragon,' Filbert said. 'Dragons live to be at least five hundred and they have to go to school for sixty years.'

'Do you have lessons?' Daniel asked. 'And homework?'

'Yes,' sighed Gilbert. 'We have lessons and homework. We have *lots* and *lots* of homework.'

'What do you learn?'

'The usual dragon things: Flying, Hovering, Hiding in Clouds, Breathing Fire.'

'That sounds great!' said Daniel. 'I wish I could learn how to breathe fire instead of doing Maths.'

'Oh, Maths is *easy*,' said Filbert. 'It only takes a week to learn Maths. Learning how to breathe fire takes ages. We've been practising for years and it's still only Zilbert who knows how to do it.'

'What are your teachers like?'

'Awful!' cried Gilbert.

'Ghastly!' exclaimed Filbert.

'Appalling!' hissed Zilbert.

'Not very nice at all,' muttered Dud.

'The worst one's Mr Catastrophe,' said Filbert. 'He teaches Hiding in Clouds. He's always losing his temper.'

'Mrs Avalanche is worse,' said Zilbert. 'She teaches Breathing Fire and she gets furious if your claws aren't sharp enough.'

'Why do you need sharp claws to breathe fire?' asked Daniel.

'You don't,' said Zilbert. 'But she always says,

"A sharp-clawed dragon is a proper dragon." And if you try and argue with her, you have to stand in a bucket of cold water for half an hour.'

'And dragons *hate* cold water!' cried all four dragons together.

'Isn't there *anything* you like learning?' Daniel asked.

'Well, we did start Invisible lessons once,' Filbert said. 'That was great. But then we stopped. That's the trouble with school. Every time you start learning something you like, they stop it and teach you something boring.'

'I didn't know dragons were invisible,' said Daniel.

'And when was the last time you saw one?' Zilbert demanded.

'I've *never* seen one.'

'There you are, then,' said Zilbert. 'That proves it.'

'But I can see you now,' said Daniel.

The dragons fell silent. They shuffled their wings and looked at the ground and twisted their tails into knots.

'Well, you see,' said Gilbert, sounding very

embarrassed, 'we know how to *become* invisible, but we don't know how to *stay* invisible. There we were, flying along, stopping to make faces at cats – cats can see a dragon even if it's invisible, you know – when Dud began to appear.'

'It's *always* Dud,' said Zilbert.

'I didn't mean to,' Dud moaned. 'I'm just not very good at some things.'

'You're not very good at *anything*,' said Zilbert.

Dud lowered his head and covered the tip of his nose with his wings.

'Then we *all* started to appear,' said Filbert. 'So we hid in this tree.'

'But what were you doing *here*?' Daniel asked. 'In *this* town?'

'We've come to find the Explorer and get *The Spelldocious* back,' said Gilbert.

'What's a Spelldocious?' Daniel asked. 'Who's the Explorer?'

Gilbert started to reply but before he could, the back door opened and Aunt Severe called out, 'Daniel! Come inside. We have to go to the supermarket.'

All four dragons jumped out of the tree and started folding up their wings.

'Where are you going?' Daniel asked.

'Shopping,' replied Gilbert. 'With you.'

'But you can't!' said Daniel. 'You mustn't let Aunt Severe see you. She's even worse than your teachers.'

'But she won't see us,' Filbert replied. 'Because we'll be invisible.'

'And besides,' Gilbert added, 'we've never seen a supermarket before.'

'So we're going,' Zilbert said.

Filbert recited the spell that made each dragon invisible.

'I thought you said you couldn't stay invisible,' Daniel said.

'Well, not for long,' Filbert agreed.

'But definitely long enough for a trip to a supermarket,' Gilbert said.

'After all,' Zilbert asked, 'what could go wrong?'

And before Daniel could object any more, they hurried him through the house and out to the front gate where Aunt Severe was waiting.

And nothing did go wrong.

Until the dragons stepped *inside* the supermarket.

8
How Rude!

The trouble began when Aunt Severe told Daniel to fetch a bag of flour. As he set off, he bumped into a woman pushing a trolley.

'You silly little boy!' she barked. 'Why don't you look where you're going?'

She pushed him aside and stormed off. Zilbert watched her go.

'How rude!' he muttered. 'Somebody ought to teach her a lesson.'

He followed her along the aisle, waited until she glanced away, then took all the tins out of her trolley and stacked them on the ground. When she turned back and saw the empty trolley, she frowned, muttered, 'Well, *really!*' and put everything back. The second she looked away, Zilbert emptied everything out again.

'Oh, this is ridiculous!' she fumed when she turned back.

Zilbert was completely invisible, so she couldn't see anything except an empty trolley in front of her.

This time, Zilbert didn't wait for her to look away. He filled the trolley with tins of custard and spun it in circles with the tip of his tail.

When the woman saw it spinning around all by itself, she grabbed the handle and tried to walk away. Zilbert held tight to his end. The woman pulled as hard as she possibly could but still the trolley wouldn't move. Then Zilbert let go. The woman and the trolley flew backwards into a freezer full of pizzas.

Zilbert dashed to her side as she jumped out. 'Oh,' he said, 'you must be cold. Let me warm you up.'

He blew little puffs of fire at the ground beneath her feet until the soles of her shoes began to smoke and melt.

This was too much for the shopper. First the trolley had emptied itself and spun round in circles. Now flames were appearing out of thin air right in front of her. And her feet were on fire!

She let out a shriek, jumped out of her shoes and raced away from the supermarket barefoot.

Zilbert clapped his claws together in satisfaction and set off to find his friends.

9
Doughnuts and Fans

Over at the bakery counter, Gilbert had just blown the baker's hat off his head with a little gust of hot air. As soon as the baker bent down to pick it up, Gilbert, Filbert and Dud sucked all the doughnuts off two trays sitting on the counter. If anybody had been watching, they would have seen forty doughnuts flying through the air and then disappearing as they vanished into the dragons' mouths.

But nobody did notice, not even Daniel, who kept looking around for a sign of the dragons as he followed Aunt Severe round the supermarket.

'Marvellous!' said Gilbert, licking his lips. 'But I'm still hungry.'

'I saw sacks of charcoal beside the front door,' said Filbert.

Off they raced. Zilbert joined them on the way. All four of them crouched down behind the pile of sacks and polished off a whole bag each. Then they looked around for something new to do.

It didn't take them long to find it.

Up on the ceiling was a large wooden fan with four wide blades whirling slowly round and round. With great big grins, the dragons unfolded their wings and galloped down the aisle.

Up they went, up over the shelves and the shoppers and dug their claws onto the end of the blades of the fan. Then they spread their wings out as wide as they would go and whirled around happily in slow, lazy circles.

All except for Dud.

He couldn't even get off the ground.

The most he could manage was to jump up and down and flap his wings furiously. But it didn't do any good. As hard as he tried he just couldn't take off.

And because he was concentrating so hard on

trying to fly, he didn't see the fruit and vegetable stand directly in front of him.

He ran headfirst right into it.

Oranges, apples, potatoes and carrots, cabbages, lettuce and grapefruit went flying. Shoppers were showered in juice and pips. And right in the middle of it all sat Dud, shaking his head and pulling bits of broken watermelon out of his ears.

Up on the fan, when he saw what had happened, Gilbert was the first to start giggling.

He couldn't help himself. That made Filbert and Zilbert start, too. But the moment they did that, they stopped holding onto the fan blades and went spinning away through the air.

Gilbert sailed into the ice-cream freezer.

Filbert flopped onto the fish counter.

Zilbert landed with an ear-splitting crash in the middle of a stack of baked beans cans.

Silence fell on the supermarket.

Then a little girl pointed at the ice-cream freezer and said, 'What's *that* funny thing?'

With a sinking heart, Daniel realized that the dragons had become visible again. What was worse was that people came running from all over the supermarket to see the dragons, who went on slipping and sliding and falling over in the ice cream and the fish and the baked beans cans as they tried to stand up straight. Soon the dragons were surrounded by shoppers staring and pointing and taking pictures with their mobile phones.

And then, before Daniel could go to the aid of his new friends, a voice boomed out, 'NOBODY MOVE!'

10
Gotcha Grabber

The voice was so loud that everybody in the supermarket stopped what they were doing immediately. Everybody except seven hulking figures who marched down the aisle, clapped their hands on Gilbert, Filbert and Zilbert, and in less than a minute had them tied up tight and bundled together on the floor.

One of the seven stood by and watched the others working. Daniel ran straight up to him.

'Who are you?' he demanded.

'Gotcha Grabber,' replied the man. He wore filthy overalls and dirty Wellington boots. He was covered from head to foot in bits of straw.

'And these,' he continued, pointing at the six

men holding the dragons captive, 'are my sons: Growler, Grappler, Guzzler, Gloater, Grinner and Gripper.'

'What are you going to do?'

'Take these weird creatures back to our zoo.'

Gotcha Grabber handed Daniel a greasy business card. It was covered in bits of old porridge. It said:

GRABBER'S
THE WORLD'S SMALLEST ZOO

Gotcha Grabber

See the animals the Grabbers has got!

Gotcha Grabber grabbed the card back and stuffed it in his pocket.

'But you can't take them away,' Daniel said. 'They don't belong to you!'

'They do now,' replied Gotcha Grabber. 'And they're going to make us tons of money. People will come from everywhere to see them.'

35

Daniel didn't have time to say another word, because right then Aunt Severe marched up the aisle and grabbed him by the arm.

'There you are!' she said. 'I've been looking everywhere for you!'

As she dragged Daniel away out of the supermarket, he glanced over his shoulder and saw Gotcha Grabber and his sons carrying Gilbert, Filbert and Zilbert off to their zoo.

That was when Daniel had a sudden thought.

What had happened to Dud? He couldn't see him anywhere.

11
The Explorer

As soon as he could when he got back home, Daniel raced out into the garden. It wasn't hard to find out where Dud had gone. There were big scratches all over the trunk where he had climbed up into the oak tree. He'd had to do it all on his own this time. There hadn't been any friends to help him. He was perched on a branch with bruises on his elbows and a cut on his nose, looking very gloomy indeed.

'Now we're *really* in trouble,' sighed the little dragon.

'I know,' said Daniel. 'I don't know how we're going to rescue Gilbert, Filbert and Zilbert.'

'I didn't mean that,' said Dud. 'I meant I can't find the Explorer on my own.'

'Who's the Explorer?' asked Daniel. 'And what was that *Spelldocious* thing Gilbert mentioned?'

So Dud explained.

'Dragons live on the other side of the world,' he began, 'in a big volcano in the middle of a huge forest. And years and years ago, when Gilbert and Filbert and Zilbert and I were all really little, an explorer discovered us by accident. We don't remember who it was but we do know that was when the trouble started.

'You see, dragons keep their spells in a big book called *The Spelldocious*. There are two copies. One is for lessons. The other is always kept locked up. The Explorer asked to see *The Spelldocious*, but humans aren't allowed to touch it because it's packed with all sorts of secret information only dragons are allowed to read. So the Explorer took a copy and ran away. Without knowing there was a spell on it.'

'A spell?'

'It makes the person who touches it forget everything.'

'Everything?'

'Well, everything about dragons,' said Dud. 'Perhaps other things, too. I don't know. But what I do know is that the Explorer lives here.'

'In this town?' said Daniel.

'In this street,' said Dud.

Daniel was dumbfounded. 'Are you sure?'

'Oh, yes. Our parents wrote the Explorer's address down. They're very careful about things like that. We copied it into the second *Spelldocious* before we ran away.'

'So *that's* why you came here,' said Daniel.

'Yes,' said Dud. 'We thought if we rescued the first *Spelldocious*, nobody would be angry with us for playing truant.'

'Which house is it? Who lives there?'

'That's the problem,' Dud sighed. 'I don't remember. I know it was this street but not which house. Or who lives there. And I can't check, either.'

'Why not?'

'Because I dropped the second *Spelldocious* down a chimney on the way here and it got burned up.' Dud hung his head and a tear fell from his eye. 'I'm *useless*,' he sighed. 'All the others are good at things. Zilbert can breathe fire. Filbert can read. *Everybody* likes Gilbert. But all *I* am is useless. I'll *never* make my name longer.'

'Longer?' asked Daniel.

'All dragons can add *'bert'* to their name when they learn to fly. It's an honour. Every dragon looks forward to it.'

'You can't fly?'

'Not yet.'

'How did you get here if you can't fly?'

'The others helped me. Like they always have to do. That's why they call me Dud, not Dudley. Because I *am* a dud,' he sobbed, letting out a second sigh that shook his whole body from nose to tail.

Daniel thought for a moment. 'Well, you did do something they couldn't do.'

'What?'

'You remembered how to stay invisible. If you hadn't done that, you wouldn't have been able to escape from the supermarket and you'd *all* be locked up in Gotcha Grabber's zoo. Then you'd really be in trouble. I think you ought to be proud of yourself.'

Dud lifted his head. 'Honestly?' he asked.

'Honestly,' said Daniel.

For the first time since Daniel had met him, Dud actually looked happy.

'Do you know how to break the spell on the Explorer?' Daniel asked.

'Oh, that's easy,' Dud said. 'All you have to be is a dragon, and introduce yourself.'

'Then let's go and do it,' said Daniel.

'But I don't know where to go,' said Dud.

'I do,' said Daniel. 'It's easy! The Explorer's called The Colonel. He told me he's forgotten his name and hasn't been able to remember it for years. *And* he's got a statue of a dragon in his front garden. I'll bet dragons are the reason he went exploring in the first place.'

Without another word, Dudley jumped down from the tree and they set off for the Colonel's house.

12
Attacked By Cats

But no sooner had they stepped out onto the pavement in front of Aunt Severe's house than Dud began glancing fearfully across the street.

'Daniel,' he whispered. 'There's a cat watching us.'

'Is that bad?' asked Daniel.

'It certainly is,' Dud replied. 'Cats don't like dragons and we don't like cats. One of them chased me when I ran away from the supermarket. I think I only got away because he went to get his friends.'

'Well, let's keep going,' said Daniel. 'We're nearly there.'

But it looked as though Dud had been right

about the cat going to tell his friends. Before they'd gone another five paces, a second cat jumped up on a gatepost beside them and let out a growl. A moment later, two more popped up behind it and a fourth and fifth climbed onto the roof of a car.

'Oh, dear!' said Dud, beginning to quiver with fear. 'Oh, dear! It's the one who chased me into your garden.'

Directly in front of them, an enormous tabby crept into view and crouched down on the pavement. It looked at Daniel. It looked at Dud. Then it sprang into the air and sank its claws deep into Dud's ankle.

And all the cats in the street joined in.

They bit Dud's tail. They nipped at his heels. They climbed up onto his shoulders and clawed at his ears. As fast as Daniel knocked them off, they jumped back up again. So he grabbed Dud's paw and ran.

They reached the Colonel's gate and dashed up the path towards his front door. By this time, Dud was covered from head to tail in cats of all colours and could barely move one foot in front of the other. When one of them covered his eyes with its paws, he ran straight into a tree. It looked as if they'd never make it.

With a mighty crash, the front door burst open and the Colonel strode into view.

In one hand he held a feather duster. In the other he brandished an umbrella. He used them both to send cats flying in every direction. Then he picked Daniel up under one arm and Dud under the other, carried them back inside and slammed the door shut behind him.

'Polish my monocle!' he said, brushing cat fur from his jacket. '*That* was a close thing!'

'Thank you, Colonel,' said Daniel. 'You were just in time.'

'Only too glad to help, young Daniel,' the Colonel replied. Then he turned towards Dud and said, 'I don't believe we've been introduced.'

'I'm Dud,' said Dud. 'I'm a dragon.'

The Colonel clapped his hands together. 'Chop my walking stick in two! So you are!'

Daniel and Dud couldn't contain their excitement.

'The spell worked!' they cried. 'He *remembers*!'

Then the Colonel showed them into his living room and what they saw inside made them stop and stare in amazement.

13
The Colonel's Plan

The room was packed from floor to ceiling with Aunt Severe's vases, trays and blankets. They were stacked on bookshelves and tables, on chairs and windowsills and all over the floor. There were so many of them that there wasn't anywhere at all to sit, so Dud perched on a pile of blankets and Daniel stood in front of the fireplace. That was when he saw the photographs on the mantelpiece.

They showed the Colonel as a young man in his uniform. In one of them, he was standing next to a young woman. She was smiling happily at the Colonel, who'd obviously just said something very funny and the two of them looked as if they were both about to burst into a fit of giggles. The woman reminded Daniel of someone, but he couldn't think who.

'Colonel,' he asked, 'who's that lady in the photographs?'

'My fiancée,' the Colonel replied. 'Splendid woman.'

But he looked very sad when he said that, so Daniel changed the subject and pointed at the map of the world on the other wall. It was covered in blue pins.

'Do the blue pins show all the places you've visited?' he asked.

'They most certainly do,' replied the Colonel. 'When I was in the Army.'

'My parents were explorers, too,' Daniel said. He told the Colonel and Dud how they'd gone missing and why he'd come to live with his aunt.

'That's terrible,' Dud said. 'Don't you have any idea where they went?'

'They said they were going to visit a forest where the trees didn't just grow out of the ground but out of the cliffs and between rocks and even at the bottom of an enormous waterfall. That's the last thing they said they were going to see.'

'And you never heard from them again?' asked Dud.

Daniel shook his head and looked glum. That made Dud glum, too, so the Colonel clapped his hands and said, 'Who'd like a glass of milk?'

'May I have a lump of coal instead?' Dud asked.

'Knot my socks together!' the Colonel said. 'Coal?'

'If you have some,' said Dud.

The Colonel pointed at the coal scuttle beside the fireplace. 'Is that enough? I'm not quite sure how much coal a dragon can eat.'

'It's perfect!' said Dud, popping a lump into his mouth and crunching it up happily.

'Cut my bow tie in half!' the Colonel exclaimed. 'I thought you were joking.'

'Oh,' said Dud, 'dragons *never* joke about coal.'

Then Daniel told the Colonel about the dragons and Gotcha Grabber and what had happened in the supermarket.

'Kidnapped?' the Colonel exclaimed. 'And by that gang of ruffians? We must take action at once!'

He grabbed his hat and his best walking stick and flung open the front door.

'Come on!' he said. 'There isn't a moment to lose!'

'Where are we going?' asked Daniel and Dud.

'To the zoo, of course,' said the Colonel. 'To rescue your friends!'

14
Two New Prisoners

Gotcha Grabber's zoo was actually just on the other side of the fence at the bottom of the Colonel's garden. It would have been quite easy to climb over the fence and get in that way. But the Colonel decided it was best to buy a ticket first and have a look at the dragons like everyone else before attempting a rescue.

So Daniel and the Colonel walked all the way along the street to join the queue of townspeople waiting to see the dragons. Dud stayed behind because he didn't want to be chased by cats again. He climbed all the way to the top of the Colonel's house and looked at the zoo from there.

Once inside the zoo, Daniel stared sadly around him. He didn't think he had ever seen such a miserable-looking place in all his life. Everywhere he looked he saw animals of all sizes, shapes and kinds jammed together as tight as marbles in a bag.

The monkeys shared a cage with the parrots and giraffes. A gloomy-looking elephant carried a crate of baboons on his back and baskets of small owls strapped to each leg. The camels lived with the ostriches, the porcupines and the kangaroos. The porcupines walked around under the camels and ostriches. The kangaroos jumped over them all.

In a corner lay a dirty pool of water. It was home to six sad penguins, a couple of crocodiles and a hippopotamus. When the hippo stood up, the penguins jumped into the water and the crocodiles unwrapped their tails and stretched out to their full length. But when the hippo decided to sit back down, the crocodiles rolled themselves into tight little balls to avoid being squashed and the penguins shot out of the water like corks from a bottle.

Right in the centre of the zoo, in an old crumbling bandstand covered from top to bottom with fishing nets and ropes and chains fastened tight with six enormous padlocks so they couldn't fly away, sat Gilbert, Filbert and Zilbert. They huddled together on the floor with their wings over their heads, their tails around their feet and their noses pointed at the ground.

The baseball cap, the umbrella and the scarf lay in a heap on the ground outside the cage.

'Turn my hat inside out!' said the Colonel. 'This place is worse than I remembered.'

'Have you been here before?' asked Daniel.

'Yes,' said the Colonel. 'I told that ruffian

Grabber he ought to give these animals some proper cages. Do you know what he told me?'

Daniel shook his head.

'He said they didn't deserve it because they were stupid. And do you know why he said they were stupid?'

Daniel shook his head a second time.

'Because they couldn't play Catch. And to prove it, he got all those wretched sons of his to bounce balls into all the cages.'

'What happened?' asked Daniel.

'Nothing, of course,' replied the Colonel. 'But the Grabbers think Catch is easy to play. So if somebody can't play it, then they must be stupid. I tell you, Daniel,' he continued, 'once we rescue young Dud's friends, I've a good mind to come back and set all these poor animals free.'

That sounded like an excellent idea to Daniel. 'May I come and help?' he asked.

But before the Colonel could open his mouth to reply, an enormous hairy hand descended on Daniel's shoulder, another gripped his arm and he was lifted off his feet into the air.

'Oo's going to let my animals *go*?' demanded

Gotcha Grabber, waving Daniel back and forth.

The Colonel tried to protect him, but Grabber's six sons picked him up and held him over their heads.

'You heard them, didn't you, boys?' boomed Gotcha Grabber. 'They was planning to steal our dragons.'

'We 'eard them, Dad!' yelled Growler, Gloater, Grinner, Grappler, Gripper and Guzzler.

'What do we do with thieves?' demanded Gotcha Grabber.

'We lock 'em up, Dad!' replied his sons.

Daniel and the Colonel were promptly carried across to the old bandstand and flung inside next to the dragons. Gotcha Grabber closed and locked all six padlocks and then the Grabbers walked away clapping their hands and patting each other on the back.

Back in the Colonel's house, Dud had seen everything. His heart sank all the way to his toes. He wanted to pull his wings up over his head and wait for somebody to come and sort everything out.

But he knew he couldn't do that because he was the only one left who could go for help. It was up to him to set his friends free.

He knew he couldn't do it alone, though. He would have to have some assistance. And the only person he could think of who might help him was Aunt Severe. He was sure she would once he told her that her great-nephew was locked up. He ran downstairs to go and find her.

Then he stopped. He'd forgotten something far more serious.

Before he could talk to Aunt Severe, he would have to get past the cats.

15
Pursued!

Dud tiptoed out of the house and peered down the street. There wasn't a cat in sight. Tucking in his wings and taking a deep breath, he set off. When he had taken five steps, he stopped and looked all around. The street was still empty. He took another five steps and looked around again.

He almost jumped out of his skin.

Sitting on a gatepost, eyeing him hungrily, was the same tabby that had chased him to the Colonel's house. As he watched, two more cats climbed up beside it and another three crawled out from under the nearest hedge.

Soon the little dragon was surrounded by cats

and his scales were absolutely blue with fear. His mouth was so dry he could hardly swallow. Very, very cautiously, he took one small step forward.

Then he put his head down and ran.

The cats shot off their perches in pursuit and leaped all over him.

He whacked them with his paws. He hit them with his tail. He threw himself from side to side. It didn't do any good. He couldn't dislodge a single cat. When one of them wrapped its paws over his eyes, he ran straight into a lamppost.

He sat down on the pavement with a thump, clutching his aching nose. While he was sitting there, the tabby jumped up and bit him on the ends of both ears.

And that was when he got angry.

His scales bristled. His tail trembled. His snout turned green and his eyes glowed red. He leaped to his feet, snapped open his wings with a loud crack, filled himself up with air and, for the first time in his life, blew a thick red jet of flame.

The cats shot off him like leaves blown away by the wind. Three of them flew into a dustbin. Four dived into a goldfish pond. The rest scrambled up to the top of the nearest tree and perched on the highest branch with eyes as big and round as dinner plates.

Back on the pavement, Dud slowly lowered his head. Drawing himself up to his full height and shaking his wings back into place, he set off towards Aunt Severe's house.

'And *don't*,' he said to them all over his shoulder, 'ever chase me again.'

16
The Door, The Staircase and The Drainpipe

Once he reached Aunt Severe's home, Dud went straight up to the front door and knocked twice. Aunt Severe peered out.

'Hello,' said Dud. 'I'm—'

'A silly little boy in a silly little dragon suit,' she said. 'Go away and play somewhere else!'

She shut the door before he could say another word.

Dud knocked again. Aunt Severe opened the door and batted him down the steps and into the weeds with a big broom.

'I'm not going to tell you again,' she announced. 'Find somewhere else to play!'

The door slammed shut.

But Dud refused to give up. 'She's *got* to listen to me,' he said and knocked for the third time.

A moment later, he heard a window open above him. He stepped back just in time to see Aunt Severe empty a big plastic bucket of water onto him. It drenched him from head to foot and sent him flying onto the grass.

'It's water!' he cried. 'It's water! And it's *cold*!'

He galloped frantically round the front garden, shaking himself and jumping up and down to get every last drop of the horrible, horrible stuff off his scales. When he was dry, he sat down and thought about what to do next.

'Well, if *she* won't let me in,' he said, 'I'll have to let *myself* in.'

He went to the back of the house and climbed the steps to the kitchen door. They were as old and neglected as the rest of the building and they trembled and wobbled precariously. The moment he grabbed the door handle, the entire staircase collapsed.

He was sitting in the wreckage, sneezing and

wiping his eyes when Aunt Severe opened the
back door and stared down at him.

'Look what you've done!' she cried. 'And
where's my door handle?'

It was still in Dud's paw. He stood up to return
it.

She snatched it back. 'Now run along home
this instant!'

'I can't!' cried Dud.

'Why?' demanded Aunt Severe as she went back inside. 'Do you live on the other side of the world?'

Before he could say another word she shut the door and locked it.

Dud sighed. He felt totally dejected. But just as he was about to give up, he noticed the drainpipe beside him. It led all the way up to an open window on the third floor.

He didn't hesitate. He wasn't very good at climbing but he *had* to help his friends. Grabbing it with all four paws, he began to climb.

He passed the first floor easily, then the second. But just as he was approaching his destination, the drainpipe began to tremble and shake.

With a horrendous squeal, the screws holding it tight to the wall popped loose and the entire drainpipe crashed to the ground. Dud only just had time to grab the windowsill. He hung by his claws, swinging gently back and forth.

Then he heard a door open.

'I wouldn't be surprised,' muttered Aunt Severe to herself as she crossed the room to the open window, 'if that beastly little boy doesn't try to climb in here next.'

She shut the window and locked it and walked away without a backward glance.

Dud climbed wearily up onto the roof and sat down next to the chimney stack. Beside it was a door. But it was locked.

He sighed again. He was trapped. He didn't know how to fly. There was no drainpipe to climb. He certainly couldn't jump. He didn't know *what* to do.

And then he realized that the solution was right there beside him.

'Of course!' he said. 'I can climb down the *chimney*!'

17
A Visit From The Fire Brigade

Dud decided that the best way to climb down the chimney was backwards. He knew he wouldn't be able to see where he was going, but he thought that if he slipped and fell, it would be better to land on his bottom than on his nose.

So he set off, wiggling from side to side, inching slowly downwards. The light at the top of the chimney grew smaller. The light beneath him grew brighter. After five minutes, he couldn't feel any more bricks with the tip of his tail. That meant that he had almost reached the bottom. A few more feet and he'd be free.

But those few feet might just as well have been miles, because no matter how hard he tried, he couldn't go any lower. He pushed and squeezed and he sucked in his stomach and shook himself up and down but none of it did any good.

He was stuck.

But he wasn't scared. After all, he'd frightened away the cats, so there was no reason why he couldn't escape from *this* predicament. And thinking about scaring the cats made him realize just how to do it. He would blow himself out of the chimney with fire. It would be just like a rocket taking off, only this time he would be going *down* instead of *up*.

He blew a thick jet of smoky red fire straight up through the chimney and into the sky. The sound made his ears rattle and his teeth shake, but it worked. He moved a few inches downwards. So he did it again. And again. And inch by inch, he moved down the chimney towards freedom.

But while he was busy escaping, a neighbour on the other side of the street looked out of his window and saw tongues of flame shooting out of Aunt Severe's chimney. He telephoned the Fire Brigade immediately.

Two minutes later, a fire engine screeched to a halt outside Aunt Severe's house. Firemen leaped out, grabbed hoses and ladders and raced up to the roof. The Fire Chief pounded on the door.

'What's going on *now*?' demanded Aunt Severe. 'Can't I have any peace?'

'You've got a fire in your chimney, madam,' announced the Fire Chief. 'Where's the fireplace?'

Aunt Severe showed him into the kitchen and pointed at the grate. It was completely bare and as neat as a pin.

'No,' said the Chief. 'I meant the one with the fire in it.'

'There's only this fireplace in the house,' replied Aunt Severe.

'Then where's the fire?' demanded the Chief.

'You're the fireman,' replied Aunt Severe. 'You tell me.'

The Chief looked up the chimney.

He didn't see a thing because Dud had heard the noise in the kitchen and made himself invisible. All the Chief saw were the firemen on the roof peering down at him.

'Let's give it a burst of water anyway,' he shouted up to them. 'And see what happens.'

The fireman on the roof turned his hosepipe on full blast. The water hit Dud on the top of his head and blew him straight out of the chimney. Still invisible, he shot between the Fire Chief's legs, rolled under the kitchen table and finished up upside down with his tail wrapped around his neck.

The Fire Chief turned to Aunt Severe. 'That's done the trick, madam,' he said. 'The fire's definitely out now.'

But Aunt Severe wasn't going to let him leave so easily. She produced a mop and a bucket and made him clean up all the water and soot on the kitchen floor. While he was doing that, she went outside and made the firemen sweep up the front path. Then she made each of them buy a tray, a vase and a blanket.

The fire engine roared away faster than it had arrived.

Aunt Severe watched it go, then went back to the kitchen and got one of the biggest shocks of her life.

Sitting in the middle of the floor, covered from nose to tail in soot and dripping dirty water everywhere, was Dud. He gave her a shy little smile and wiped the end of his nose with his paw.

'Hello,' he sniffed. 'I'm a dragon. My name's Dudley.'

18

How The Colonel Forgot His Name

Back in the bandstand, everybody was feeling very, very gloomy. Everyone except the Colonel.

'Come on,' he said. 'Cheer up! I've been in trickier spots than this, you know. Why, once I was trapped in a snowstorm for twenty years.'

The dragons and Daniel stared at him in disbelief.

'It happened,' he explained, 'when I was sent to guard a castle high up in the mountains on the other side of the world. But no sooner had we arrived than it began to snow. It snowed all day and all night and every day and night after for two whole months. When it was finished, there was no way up to the castle and no way down. We were trapped.'

'What did you do?' asked Daniel.

'First we tried to radio for help, but that was no good because the radio was frozen solid. Then we tried to telephone for help, but that was no good because the telephone lines had fallen down. We tried digging our way out, but the snow was so deep we couldn't see which way to go and went round in circles. So we decided to stay in the castle and wait for the snow to melt. But it didn't melt. Not for the first year, nor for the second, the third or the fourth. In fact, it didn't melt for the next twenty years. That was how we forgot our names.'

'You can't forget your name,' said Gilbert.

'We haven't forgotten *our* names,' said Filbert and Zilbert.

'That's because you use them every day,' the Colonel said. 'You say "Hello, Filbert" or "Bye bye, Gilbert" or "Where are you going, Zilbert?" But when you're a soldier, you say *"Good morning, Sergeant"* and he says, *"Good morning, Colonel."* Or you say, *"Time to see how deep that snow is, Corporal"* and he replies *"Right away, sir."* By the

72

time the snow finally melted and we were able to leave, we were so used to doing without our names that we'd forgotten them completely.'

'Didn't the Army tell you when you got home?' asked Daniel.

'They'd forgotten all about us,' the Colonel said.

'What about your fiancée?' asked Daniel. 'I don't see how *she* could have forgotten.'

The Colonel's good spirits vanished in a second.

'She didn't even recognize me,' he sighed. 'She said she'd never met me before in her life.'

'That's awful,' said Daniel.

'Yes, it is,' agreed the Colonel. 'But I wasn't about to give up. I decided that if she didn't remember me, I'd buy a house as close to hers as I could find and wait until she did.'

'Do you mean she lives near here?' asked Daniel. 'Have I seen her?'

'Of course you've seen her,' said the Colonel. 'She's your great-aunt.'

Daniel was astounded. 'Aunt Severe was your fiancée? The woman in the photographs?

I thought she looked familiar.'

'Well, that's not her real name,' said the Colonel. 'Her real name is Emily Florence Biddle-Smith. But I called her Giggleswick. Because she certainly used to do a lot of giggling when she was young.'

'Giggle?' said Daniel. 'Aunt Severe giggled?'

'You could hardly get her to stop,' said the Colonel. 'My sides used to ache from all the giggling we did.'

'So is that why you buy everything she makes?'

'Of course,' said the Colonel. 'It's the only time I get to talk to her.'

But Daniel was puzzled by something. 'Colonel,' he asked, 'when did you find the dragons?'

'Dragons?' said the Colonel, looking just as puzzled.

'When did you stay with them and run away with *The Spelldocious* and lose your memory? Did you do that after the snow melted, when you left the castle?'

The Colonel looked even more puzzled. 'I'm

afraid I haven't the slightest idea what you're talking about.'

So Daniel explained all about the Explorer and *The Spelldocious* and the dragons.

'Fill my overcoat with moths!' the Colonel exclaimed when Daniel was finished. 'Do you mean to tell me that Gilbert, Filbert, Zilbert and Dud are *real* dragons?'

'We most certainly are,' said Gilbert.

'I thought you were just children dressed up in dragon suits who'd been kidnapped,' the Colonel said. 'That's why I was so surprised when young Dud ate a lump of coal.'

'You gave Dud some coal?' Gilbert asked.

'Have you got any more with you?' Filbert enquired.

'I'm starving!' said Zilbert.

The Colonel shook his head and then everybody sat there in silence until Filbert spoke.

'The Colonel can't be the Explorer,' she said.

'If he was the Explorer,' Gilbert added, 'he would have remembered where *The Spelldocious* was when Dud introduced himself.'

'Well if he's not the Explorer,' Zilbert demanded, 'who is?'

'I know,' Daniel said, very quietly.

Everyone turned to look at him.

'Who else on that street doesn't remember things?' he asked. 'She certainly doesn't remember that the Colonel was her fiancé.'

Nobody in the bandstand said a word.

'Yes,' said Daniel. 'Aunt Severe.'

19
The Spelldocious

The moment Dud announced his name and told her he was a dragon, Aunt Severe sat down on the floor with a bump. Her big grey skirts went flying up around her head and her hat flew off.

'Oh dear,' she said in a faint little voice. 'Oh dear!'

'I'm sorry if I scared you,' said Dud. 'I didn't mean to.'

'Oh, I'm not scared,' she said. 'I've just remembered. After all these years, I've just remembered *everything*!'

She clambered to her feet, took Dud by the paw and led him all the way up to the room at the top of the house where she'd stored Daniel's books and toys. Once inside, she stopped in front of a large trunk. When she lifted the lid, the hinges creaked and clouds of dust billowed up into the air. The two of them peered inside.

Lying at the bottom was a thick, leather-bound book covered in strange symbols and figures.

'It's *The Spelldocious*!' Dud whispered.

'Yes,' said Aunt Severe. 'It's *The Spelldocious*. And I stole it. I'd been all over the world looking for my fiancé, you know. He'd gone away with the Army and been missing for years. I didn't mean to find you dragons at all. When I heard about *The Spelldocious*, I thought I'd be able to use it to find him. That's the only reason I took it. But there must have been a spell on it, I suppose.'

'Yes,' said Dud and told her all about it and how the spell had now been broken because she'd been introduced to a dragon.

'Well,' she said, 'I certainly remember it all now. I even remember you.'

'You remember me?' gasped Dud.

'I remember you when you were very, very little,' said Aunt Severe. 'And your friends. There's Gil, who thinks he knows everything and Fil who really does. And then, of course, there's Zil with that terrible temper of his.'

'They're Gilbert, Filbert and Zilbert now.'

Aunt Severe looked around. 'Where are they, by the way?'

So Dud told her everything that had happened from the moment the dragons had hidden in the tree in the garden, all the way up to his appearance in the kitchen.

Aunt Severe was aghast. 'Those frightful Grabbers have locked up my great-*nephew*?' she boomed.

She picked up *The Spelldocious* and set off downstairs. Dud raced after her.

'Where are we going?' he asked.

'To get them back, of course. Now, I want you to fly over the zoo. The moment those Grabbers see another dragon, they'll chase after you and that will give me time to get inside and rescue everyone.'

'That won't work,' said Dud, hanging his head in shame.

'Why ever not?' demanded Aunt Severe.

'Because I can't fly,' he replied.

'Didn't you tell me,' said Aunt Severe, 'that you came here with Gilbert, Filbert and Zilbert?'

'Yes.'

'Then you must be Dudleybert.'

'No,' Dud said. 'I'm just not good at it. I'm not very good at anything, really.'

'Nonsense!' said Aunt Severe. 'You got into

80

this house. Everybody else would have given up before they thought about climbing down the chimney. You strike me as a most clever and resourceful young dragon.'

The way she said it made Dud feel wonderful. But only for a moment. 'I still can't fly,' he muttered.

'Then we shall go outside and have a lesson.'

But a lesson didn't do any good. No matter how much he tried, Dud still couldn't stay in the air for more than a couple of seconds.

Aunt Severe frowned. 'Well, we've got to get them out of the zoo somehow,' she said.

That was when Dud had a brainwave. 'Have you got any balloons?' he asked.

'*Balloons?*' said Aunt Severe, looking very puzzled.

'If you've got balloons,' Dud said, 'I *can* get a dragon to fly.'

20
A Flying Dragon

So they bought balloons. Hundreds of them. 232, to be precise. Dud filled them practically to bursting with gusts of hot dragon breath and Aunt Severe attached them with string to every part of the statue of the dragon in the Colonel's front garden.

They floated from its nose and its tail, from its back legs and its forearms, from its stomach and its back and its ears. Soon there were so many balloons the statue could hardly be seen. But they got over that problem by finding just the right spell in *The Spelldocious* to make the balloons vanish from sight.

And then all they had to do was let the statue go.

Up and away it drifted, over the trees and out across the town, looking *exactly* like a living, breathing dragon gliding gently through the sky.

Aunt Severe and invisible Dud raced all the way round to the zoo and reached the front gates just as the statue passed overhead.

'A dragon!' Aunt Severe cried. 'There goes another dragon!'

Gotcha Grabber and his sons took one look and then they grabbed ropes, chains and nets and roared off through the town in hot pursuit of the statue. When they were out of sight, Aunt Severe hurried into the zoo and up to the bandstand. Dud followed along behind.

Everyone was delighted to see her – the Colonel most of all – but Aunt Severe didn't seem pleased to see them. She fixed them with her most forbidding glare. Then she surveyed the six big padlocks.

'Since,' she announced, 'I don't have a key to open these locks, I will open them with a spell. I shall require silence while I work.'

She opened *The Spelldocious* and began to read. The words she spoke sounded like somebody squashing a lot of eggs in a box filled with custard.

When she'd finished, the Colonel turned into a bowl of jelly.

Gilbert stuck his claw into it and licked it. 'Hmm,' he said. 'Strawberry.'

Aunt Severe frowned and tried again.

The Colonel stayed a bowl of jelly but Daniel turned into a lump of coal.

Zilbert popped it into his mouth.

'That's *Daniel*,' Filbert said, reaching into his mouth and plucking the lump free before Zilbert could crunch it up.

'But I'm *hungry*,' Zilbert grumbled.

He fell silent as Aunt Severe recited spell number three.

The roof of the bandstand blew off. The dragons shot into the air. The Colonel turned back into the Colonel, and Daniel turned back into Daniel. Everyone landed on the grass with a thump.

'Tie my shirt sleeves together,' muttered the Colonel, wriggling around inside his clothes. 'I'm sticky.'

'And I'm covered in coal,' said Daniel.

'We're *dizzy*,' said the dragons, clutching their stomachs.

Aunt Severe slammed *The Spelldocious* shut. 'No time for complaining!' she commanded. 'Follow me.'

Daniel stayed behind to pick something up, then ran after them. Aunt Severe led everyone over to the fence separating her garden from the zoo and pulled back a loose board so everyone could crawl through. Then she took them into her house and down the passage to the kitchen where she filled the sink with water and turned to face the dragons.

'Right,' she said. 'Who's first?'

The dragons looked at the water. Then they looked at Aunt Severe.

'We're not thirsty, thank you very much,' said Filbert politely.

'Oh, it's not for *drinking*,' replied Aunt Severe.

The scales of all four dragons turned blue with fright as they realized what was about to happen.

'You're going to have a *bath*,' she announced.

21
Back To School

'Dragons,' said Gilbert politely, 'don't actually *like* water.'

'I am *not* having four grubby young dragons putting muddy claw prints all over my nice clean floors,' Aunt Severe replied sternly. 'Who's first?'

Gilbert, Filbert and Zilbert pointed at Dud. 'He is!'

Dud swallowed nervously. He hopped up onto the draining board and peered at the water. Then he took a deep breath, stepped in and sat down. His teeth chattered furiously. Aunt Severe scrubbed him from head to tail, wrapped him in a big fluffy towel and gave him a lump of coal.

'That's for being brave,' she said.

As soon as they saw the coal, the other three dragons couldn't wait to take a bath. When they were all clean, Aunt Severe lined them up in a row.

'Good,' she said. 'Now it's time for lessons. Come along.'

'Don't we get a lump of coal?' asked Gilbert.

'Whatever for?' she asked.

'For having a bath,' he said. 'You gave Dud one.'

'That's because he was first.'

Gilbert and Filbert and Zilbert were indignant. 'That's not *fair*!' they whined.

'Silence!' barked Aunt Severe and clapped her hands together with a sound like thunder. 'Upstairs, with all of you. At once!'

Once there, she made them all – even Daniel and the Colonel – sit on the floor in front of a blackboard.

'This is almost like school,' Filbert whispered to Gilbert.

'No talking!' said Aunt Severe.

Zilbert glared at the ground. 'It's *exactly* like school,' he muttered.

'Now,' continued Aunt Severe, 'you are going to learn how to tell your parents where you are. This,' she continued, drawing a line of strange shapes on the blackboard, 'is the song you are going to sing to them. Read it out loud, please, Filbert.'

Filbert did so. Then the other dragons took their turns. When they were finished, Aunt Severe made them recite it backwards, forwards and backwards again.

'Good,' she said. She pointed at the Colonel. 'Now it's your turn.'

'I beg your pardon,' said the Colonel, who was feeling very sad because Aunt Severe still hadn't recognized him.

'I *thought* you weren't paying attention,' said Aunt Severe.

'But it's in dragon language,' exclaimed the Colonel.

'That's no excuse for not paying attention!' said Aunt Severe. 'Go and stand in the corner!'

Sadly, the Colonel did as he was told. Aunt Severe turned to Daniel.

'And I suppose,' she said, 'that you're going to tell me *you* weren't listening either.'

Daniel nodded.

'Then make yourselves useful and off to the bathroom with you both!' she commanded. 'Get cleaned up like these nice dragons!'

Daniel and the Colonel trudged gloomily away.

The lesson continued. Finally, Aunt Severe was satisfied and told the dragons to go up onto the roof. As they got ready to go, she saw Zilbert step away from the blackboard with his paws behind his back. 'What,' she demanded, 'have you got there?'

Zilbert opened his paw to reveal three sticks of chalk. 'I only wanted to know what they tasted like,' he explained.

'I see,' said Aunt Severe, taking them from him and giving a piece each to Gilbert, Filbert and Dud.

They gobbled the chalk up and licked their lips.

'Was that tasty?' she enquired.

'Lovely,' said Filbert.

'Scrumptious,' said Gilbert.

'Almost better than coal,' said Dud.

Aunt Severe turned to Zilbert. 'There,' she said. 'Now you know what it tastes like.'

When everyone had left, Zilbert let out a moan.

'I was wrong,' he muttered. 'This is *worse* than school.'

22

Dud's Second Song

Once everyone was assembled on the roof, Aunt Severe told the dragons to form a circle.

'Take a deep breath,' she said.

They took a long, deep breath.

'Join paws.'

They joined their paws.

The rooftop was absolutely silent.

'And *sing*,' whispered Aunt Severe. 'The better you sing, the better your parents will hear you.'

The song the dragons sang sounded like dry leaves rustling along an empty pavement in winter. It wafted up over the trees and drifted away on the warm, evening breeze until finally, as quietly as it had begun, it faded away into silence and stopped.

Gilbert and Filbert and Zilbert lowered their heads and shook their wings. But while they were busy congratulating each other, Dud kept his head up and his eyes closed.

He began to sing again.

Immediately, all the dragons stood stock still. It is very bad manners to interrupt a dragon while he is singing.

'And what,' asked Aunt Severe when Dud finished, 'was *that* all about? I didn't understand a word of it.'

'Oh, nothing,' said Dud, putting his paws behind his back and staring at the ground. 'Can we have another piece of coal? Before our mums come and get us? We *were* good.'

Aunt Severe realized he wasn't going to tell her. 'All right,' she said. 'But only one piece. You know you can't fly if you've eaten too much.'

The dragons let out a whoop and roared away downstairs. Then the whoops stopped and the house fell silent. Not even a floorboard creaked. When Daniel, Aunt Severe and the Colonel reached the kitchen, they found out why.

Standing before them, with their hands on their hips and big grins on theirs faces, were the Grabbers. On the floor, trussed up tight in a big net, were Gilbert, Filbert, Zilbert and Dud.

'Gotcha!' said Gotcha Grabber.

23
Daniel's Challenge

'We saw you all up there standing around on the roof,' the zookeeper said. 'We couldn't miss you. Right, lads,' he said to his sons, 'get them into the lorry.'

'What lorry?' said Daniel.

'The lorry that's going to take them to the zoo I'm selling them to,' said Gotcha Grabber. 'We're going to make a fortune.'

'You can't do that!' cried Daniel.

'They're my dragons again,' said Gotcha Grabber. 'And I can do anything I want with a bunch of stupid dragons.'

When he used the word 'stupid' again, it gave Daniel an idea. 'What if we prove they're not?' he said.

'Prove they're not what?' asked Gotcha Grabber.

'Stupid,' said Daniel. 'Will you let them go if we can prove that?'

''Ow are you going to do that?'

'We'll play games. You told the Colonel animals are stupid because they can't play games.'

'That's right,' said Gotcha Grabber.

'Then let's play some games and see if it's true. If the dragons win, you let them go. If they don't, you keep them.'

Gotcha Grabber thought it over. 'All right,' he said. 'But we pick the games.'

Daniel agreed.

'The first game'll be Hide-and-Seek.'

The dragons smiled big dragon smiles when they heard that.

'The second game'll be Tiddlywinks.'

The dragons frowned. But Aunt Severe smiled.

'And the last game'll be Catch.'

The dragons looked even more alarmed at the

thought of Catch than they had at the thought of Tiddlywinks.

'But the teams aren't even,' Gotcha Grabber said. 'There are seven of us but I only see four dragons.'

Aunt Severe stepped forward. 'There are four dragons,' she said, 'plus Daniel, Daniel's friend and myself. You will play, won't you?' she asked the Colonel.

The Colonel snapped to attention. 'I most certainly shall.'

Aunt Severe smiled sweetly at the Grabbers. 'You're not scared to play games with four dragons, a little boy and two old fogies, are you?'

'No!' the Grabbers roared, with a yell that made the cups and saucers on the sideboard tremble. 'We ain't scared of anyone!'

So they all went out into the garden to play Hide-and-Seek, Tiddlywinks and Catch.

24
Hide-and-Seek

As everyone went outside, the dragons couldn't stop giggling.

'What's so funny?' Daniel whispered to Gilbert.

'When was the last time you played Hide-and-Seek with somebody who was *invisible*?' Gilbert replied. 'Those Grabbers will never find us. Oh, this is going to be so easy.'

Gilbert was right.

It *was* easy.

It was easy for the Grabbers.

They found Aunt Severe crouched behind a bramble bush with a bunch of dandelions tied to her head. The Colonel was standing next to her on one leg, trying to look like a fence post. Daniel was up in the tree, pretending to be a pear. They pulled him out in no time at all.

Then they produced big sharp sticks and poked them into every bush and patch of weeds in the garden.

Gilbert jumped out of a rose bush clutching his nose. Filbert popped up holding her tummy and Dud and Zilbert rolled out of a clump of giant stinging nettles. Being invisible didn't mean that you couldn't be poked with a stick.

And the pain certainly made you forget all about staying invisible.

But when Daniel's team started looking, they couldn't find the slightest trace of the zookeeper and his sons. They searched the garden from top to bottom and side to side and came up with nothing.

'I do believe,' said Aunt Severe after ten minutes had gone by, 'that they've won.'

No sooner were the words out of her mouth than seven grubby Grabber faces popped into view . . . on the other side of the fence.

'You're standing in the zoo!' cried Daniel. 'That's cheating.'

'Nobody said *where* we could hide,' replied Gotcha.

Everyone fell silent as Aunt Severe whacked the fence with her walking stick.

'It's time for Tiddlywinks,' she said. 'And I'm going to play for everyone on my team.'

And with that she turned to Daniel and winked.

25
Tiddlywinks

'Now,' said Aunt Severe to Gotcha Grabber. 'I am rather old, so you'll have to tell me how to play.'

'Easy,' said Gotcha Grabber. 'You flip your plastic counters into the cup. The first person to get all their counters in the cup is the winner.'

'That doesn't sound so hard,' said Aunt Severe. 'Do you mind if I play standing up?'

'How are you going to hit the counters?'

'With the end of my walking stick.'

The Grabbers grinned from ear to ear. They thought it would be easy to beat an old woman using a walking stick to play Tiddlywinks.

They didn't know how wrong they were.

Grinner was the first to play, but before he had a chance to move, Aunt Severe's walking stick flashed up and down seven times and all seven counters clattered into the cup. All the years she'd spent flicking pieces of rubbish from the gutter into the wheelbarrow had made her an expert. Grinner lumbered off to the fence to sulk.

Guzzler took his place. She beat him, too. Then she beat Gripper and after that she trounced Growler.

And then she giggled. It wasn't a very loud giggle and it didn't last very long, and as soon as it was out of her mouth she became sensible Aunt Severe again.

But it was definitely a giggle.

'Now,' she said. 'I've won four out of seven games, so your team can't possibly beat me. That means we've won and the score is One - All.'

'Huh!' snarled Gotcha Grabber. He pulled a red rubber ball from his pocket and bounced it up and down in his hands. 'Let's see how you do at Catch!'

26
Catch

Daniel and Grinner played first. Grinner thought it would be easy to beat a little boy, so he kept grinning at his brothers when he should have been concentrating on the ball. By the time he realized he wasn't paying enough attention, he'd lost three times and was out.

The Colonel went next and he beat Gloater in no time at all with a googly, a leg spinner and a bouncer.

'Cricket,' he explained when Daniel asked. 'I learned to play in the castle. I was an *excellent* bowler.'

And when Aunt Severe played, very strange things happened.

The first time the ball spun around twice in the air and shot through Gripper's fingers. The second time it stopped dead in the air before slipping between his knees and rolling away into the grass. The third time, it vanished. When Gripper finally gave up and looked away, it fell out of the air, bounced off the top of his head and rolled away into the weeds.

'How did you do *that*?' Filbert whispered.

'Oh,' replied Aunt Severe nonchalantly, 'just a little trick your mother taught me.'

Then it was the dragons' turn. In the air, dragons are swift and graceful creatures. On the ground, running backwards and forwards with their eyes fixed on a tiny little ball and trying not to trip over their tails, they are awkward and clumsy. Gilbert kept falling down. Zilbert got trapped in a tree. Filbert couldn't wrap her claws around the ball at all.

Before anyone knew it, the score was Three - All.

There was only one game left to play.

And that was between Dud and Gotcha Grabber.

Without any warning, Gotcha Grabber hurled the ball straight at his opponent. Dud ducked and it sailed over his head. But, as he ducked, his tail swung up, the ball hit it and flew back across the garden, straight past an astonished Gotcha Grabber's hands.

One – Nil to Dud.

The second time, Gotcha Grabber threw the ball at Dud's nose. Dud covered his face with his claws. The ball bounced off them and onto the ground.

One – All.

Gotcha Grabber grinned greedily. 'Get them nets ready, boys. This won't take long.'

He leaned right back until his hand almost touched the ground, then threw the ball as hard as he could straight into the air. Up, up and up it went, over the dragons, over the Colonel and Aunt Severe, over Daniel, right over Dud and straight towards the fence.

Everyone on Daniel's team groaned. They knew they had lost.

Except for Dud.

He ran towards the fence. His neck stretched

out. His tail waved from side to side. His wings unfolded and snapped into position, just as Aunt Severe had taught him. And then he took off and soared into the air.

Over the weeds and past the tree he flew with his claws outstretched in front of him. With a resounding CLACK, he wrapped them round the ball and held it tight.

Two – One . . . to Dud.

The dragons leaped up and down. Daniel yelled

and hollered. Aunt Severe waved her walking stick and gave the Colonel a great big kiss. The Colonel blushed and straightened his monocle. And directly overhead, Dud flew six somersaults in the air before swooping back down to the ground and placing the ball in Gotcha Grabber's hand.

'We've won,' he said.

'You 'ave,' replied Gotcha Grabber. He didn't look particularly sad. 'But I forgot to tell you something,' he added.

'What's that?'

'We're a bunch of cheats. Get 'em, lads!'

Out came the ropes and nets and before anybody knew it Gilbert, Filbert, Zilbert and Dud were tied up tight for the third time that day.

But before the Grabbers could carry them away, a shadow so dark it blotted out the sunlight entirely fell across the garden. A second later, three enormous jets of flame scorched the weeds to ashes. With a mighty roar of leathery wings, three full-grown dragons landed in the garden.

They stood before the oak tree, gazing down at the human figures staring back at them. Finally, their eyes settled on the bundle lying in front of Gotcha Grabber.

The largest dragon walked slowly towards it. The ground trembled under its feet. When it lowered its head and spoke, the leaves in the tree shivered and shook.

'Well, well, well,' it said, 'if it isn't little Zilbert.'

The garden was absolutely still.

Then a shy little voice replied, 'Hello, Mum.'

27

All Together Again

'You,' said Zilbert's mother, 'are a naughty little dragon.'

Zilbert's voice was so faint that it could hardly be heard. 'Yes, Mum,' he said.

'But,' she continued, 'I'm still *very* happy to see you.'

She sliced open the net with one flick of her talons and the little dragons spilled out onto the grass. They leaped straight into their mothers' arms and their mothers turned them over on their backs and breathed warm air on their tummies. All except Dud. He stood by himself looking up at the sky.

'Don't worry,' said Filbert's mum. 'She's on her way.'

And so she was. Far away in the distance appeared a familiar figure. In less than a minute it landed in the garden and Dud jumped happily into his mother's arms and rolled onto his back to have his tummy warmed up.

After a minute of this, Dud's mum set him down and looked around.

'Which one of you is Daniel?' she asked.

'I am,' said Daniel.

'Well,' said Dud's mum, 'I've brought someone to see you.'

She lowered her tail to the ground and two figures stepped slowly off her back and onto the grass. When they saw Daniel, their faces lit up with great big smiles and they scooped him up into their arms and squeezed him so tight he could hardly breathe.

'Mum!' he cried. 'Dad! Where *were* you?'

'Trapped at the top of an enormous tree, in a forest so big you couldn't see the sides of it,' said his father.

'But how did the dragons know where to look?'

'Dud told us,' said Gilbert's mother. 'After the dragons sang their song for help. That was what *he* sang.'

Daniel's mum and dad turned to Dud and shook his paw. 'Thank you very much,' they said.

Dud blushed and covered his head with his tail.

Then the dragon mothers turned their attention to Aunt Severe.

She held out *The Spelldocious*. 'I'm sorry I stole it,' she said.

Filbert's mother took it and tucked it safely away behind her wing. 'I don't think we should be too angry,' she said. 'After all, if you hadn't had this copy, you wouldn't have been able to help our little runaways, would you?'

'And talking of little runaways,' said Zilbert's mother, 'does one of you happen to have a second

Spelldocious with you?'

All four dragons hung their heads.

'Or did you lose it?' she asked.

All four dragons slowly nodded.

'Well,' Zilbert's mum said at last, 'I don't suppose that's so bad.'

All four dragons looked up expectantly.

'We've always needed more copies. So *you* can make one. Each one of you can make a copy. That should give you something to do for a while.'

All four dragons sat on the grass and let out a long sad sigh at the thought of all the hours and hours of copying waiting for them when they got home.

'Now,' Filbert's mother said, 'I know everybody here except the gentleman standing beside you. Aren't you going to introduce us?'

'I'm afraid I can't,' said Aunt Severe. 'I don't know who he is.'

Filbert's mother looked at the dragons. 'Did you say the *whole* spell?' she asked.

'We thought all we had to do was introduce ourselves,' the dragons said, looking embarrassed. 'Wasn't that enough?'

'No,' replied Filbert's mother, 'not quite. You have to tell the person under the spell their name, too.' Then she turned back to Aunt Severe and said, 'And you are Emily Florence Biddle-Smith.'

A funny look came over Aunt Severe's face. She blinked and shook her head and then she looked at the Colonel and smiled a smile so big her teeth almost popped out of her mouth.

'You're my fiancé!' she cried. ' You're my fiancé, Colonel Anthony Auchinloss Arbuthnot!'

'Well, bake my bootlaces!' the Colonel gasped. 'You've remembered my name!'

'And I've been so rotten to you,' said Aunt Severe. 'Will you ever forgive me?'

'Nothing would make me happier!' the Colonel cried and swept her into his arms for a massive hug.

'And just where do *you* lot think you're going!'

While everybody else was watching the Colonel and Aunt Severe, the Grabbers were trying to sneak away. But Zilbert's mother trapped them all with her wing.

She lowered her head to the zookeeper's face. 'Are you the man who locked up my little boy?'

Gotcha Grabber quivered and quaked in his boots. 'It was just a joke,' he said.

'Oh,' said Zilbert's mum. 'Well, in that case we've got a joke for you. You're going to come and live with us for a few years. That ought to make you laugh. It's certainly going to make *us* happy.'

She scooped all seven of them up and popped them behind her wings.

'You can't carry us like this!' shouted Gotcha Grabber. 'What if we fall off?'

'Oh, I wouldn't do that if I were you,' she replied. 'It might be dangerous.'

By then the sun was beginning to set and shadows were creeping across the garden.

'We can't stay,' said Filbert's mother. 'It's time to go.'

That was when Daniel produced the baseball cap, the umbrella and the scarf.

'I rescued them when you escaped from the bandstand,' he explained.

Gilbert, Filbert and Zilbert started to put

them on. Then they stopped and looked at each other.

And then they gave everything to Dud.

'You deserve these,' Filbert said.

'You saved us,' Gilbert added.

'Even if you didn't bring any coal with you,' Zilbert muttered.

Dud put on the cap, tied the scarf around his neck and clutched the umbrella tight in his paw. He looked very smart. And very proud.

'But what about your name?' Daniel said.

'Yes,' said Aunt Severe. 'You can fly now. You have to change your name.'

'Oh, that's easy,' Dud announced. 'It's going to be Dudbert.'

'Dudbert?' echoed his friends. 'Not Dudleybert?'

'Dudbert's my name and Dudbert I'm proud of.'

'Then Dudbert it is!' said his mother, looking very pleased with her brave young son.

Then everybody hugged everybody else and said goodbye and the dragons unfurled thei wings and began lumbering through the weed

Once again the ground shook and the garden was filled with thick dark shadows. One by one, all eight dragons took off and soared into the air. Soon there was nothing left to see in the sky except clouds.

The Colonel turned to Aunt Severe.

'What's going to happen to all the animals in the zoo?' he asked. 'We can't just leave them there.'

'We could knock down that fence at the end of our gardens,' she said, 'and the one *between* our gardens and make it all into one bigger zoo. That would keep us busy, wouldn't it?'

The Colonel clapped his hands. 'Fill my shoes with custard! What a wonderful idea! When do we start?'

'Just as soon as we've had a cup of tea.'

The grown-ups went off to the kitchen. Only Daniel remained, hoping for one last glimpse of his friends. Just as he was about to give up and go inside, something flickered in the distance. It swooped down across the garden, up over the roof and back down to hover in the air above Daniel.

It was Dud.

'I didn't say a proper goodbye,' he said. 'And I wanted to thank you for helping me. A proper thank you, just for you.'

'That's OK,' said Daniel.

'It was the best fun I've ever had,' said the little dragon.

'Me, too,' said Daniel.

'I'll miss you, Daniel,' said Dud.

'I'll miss you, too, Dud,' said Daniel. 'I hope you *can* come back one day.'

'I'll certainly try,' said the dragon. 'Goodbye, Daniel.'

'Goodbye, Dud.'

With a flap of his wings, Dud soared up over the tree. A few seconds after that, Daniel couldn't see him at all. When he turned round, he found his mother waiting for him.

'Do you want to come inside for some tea?' she asked.

Daniel took one last look at the sky and then he smiled. 'Yes,' he said. 'That would be nice.'

And the two of them went inside to join the others.